LET'S FIND OUT! *TRANSPORTATION*

ALL ABOUT SPACECRAFT

TRACY BROWN HAMILTON

Britannica
Educational Publishing

IN ASSOCIATION WITH

ROSEN
EDUCATIONAL SERVICES

Published in 2017 by Britannica Educational Publishing (a trademark of Encyclopædia Britannica, Inc.) in association with The Rosen Publishing Group, Inc.
29 East 21st Street, New York, NY 10010

Distributed exclusively by Rosen Publishing.
To see additional Britannica Educational Publishing titles, go to rosenpublishing.com.

First Edition

Britannica Educational Publishing
J.E. Luebering: Executive Director, Core Editorial
Mary Rose McCudden: Editor, Britannica Student Encyclopedia

Rosen Publishing
Christine Poolos: Editor
Nelson Sá: Art Director
Nicole Russo: Designer
Cindy Reiman: Photography Manager
Karen Huang: Photo Researcher

Library of Congress Cataloging-in-Publication Data

Names: Hamilton, Tracy Brown, author.
Title: All about spacecraft / Tracy Brown Hamilton.
Description: First edition. | New York : Britannica Educational Publishing in
association with Rosen Educational Services, [2017] | Series: Let's find out! Transportation | Includes bibliographical references and index. |
Audience: 1-4.
Identifiers: LCCN 2015050349| ISBN 9781680484458 (library bound : alk. paper)
| ISBN 9781680484533 (pbk. : alk. paper) | ISBN 9781680484229 (6-pack :
alk. paper)
Subjects: LCSH: Space vehicles--Juvenile literature. | Outer
space--Exploration--Juvenile literature.
Classification: LCC TL795 .H358 2017 | DDC 629.4--dc23
LC record available at https://lccn.loc.gov/2015050349

CONTENTS

WHY HUMANS EXPLORE SPACE

Humans have been interested in exploring, or studying, space for thousands of years. Starting in about 1600, scientists used telescopes to get a better view of the objects in the sky. Only in recent decades has it been possible to travel into space to get a closer look at the Moon and other bodies.

More than 5,000 spacecraft have been

An astronaut from the space shuttle *Challenger* floats in outer space.

launched into space to gather information since 1957. They include spacecraft with humans onboard, space probes, and satellites. The Soviet Union (now Russia) and the United States were originally the main countries exploring space. Many other countries are now involved, including China and the European countries that are part of the European Space Agency. Through space exploration humans have learned a great deal about the planets, stars, and other objects in space.

NASA's Hubble Space Telescope captured this image of stars seen in our Milky Way galaxy.

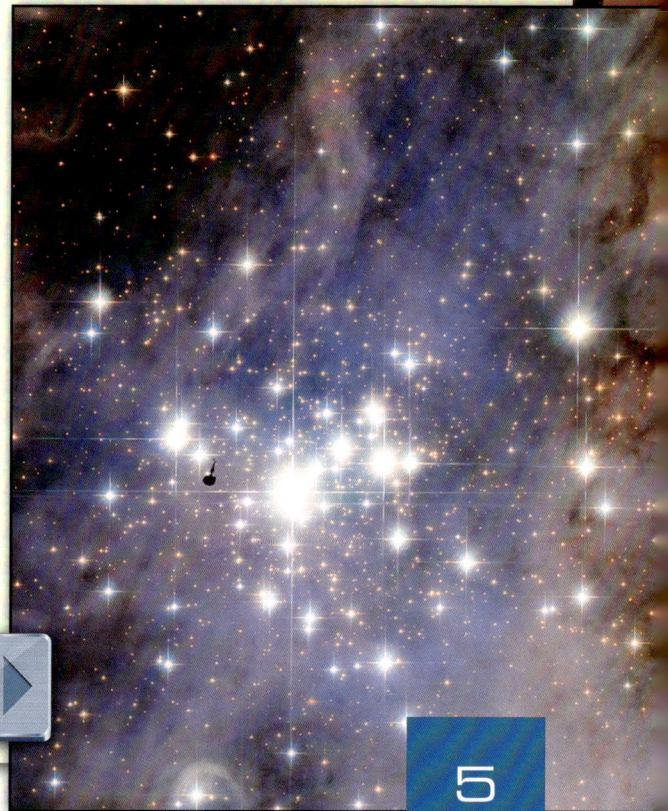

Understanding Gravity

The biggest challenge of getting objects into space is breaking through Earth's gravity. Gravity is a pulling force that works across space. It causes all objects to attract other objects. For example, the Sun, which is millions of miles from Earth, pulls on Earth and the other planets and objects in the solar system. These objects would move in a straight line, but the force of gravity pulls them toward the Sun. At the same time, the speed of the

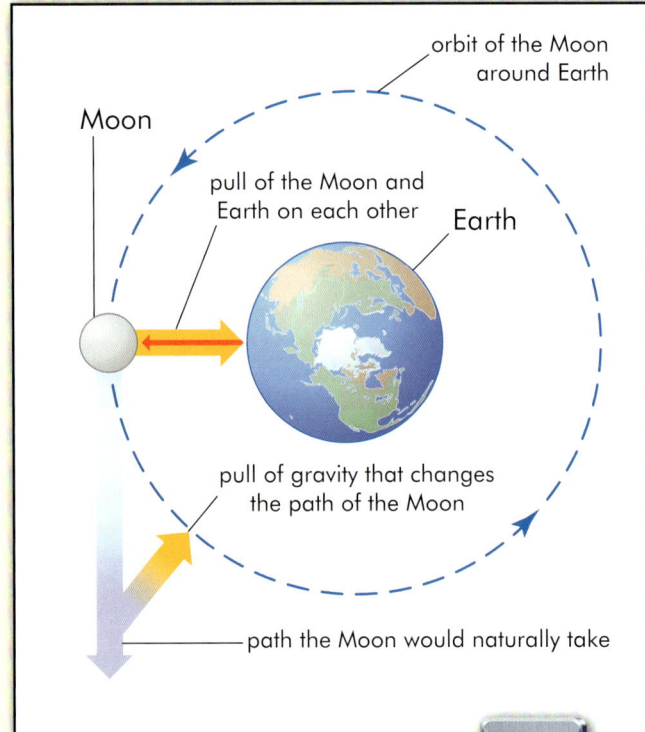

orbit of the Moon around Earth

Moon

pull of the Moon and Earth on each other

Earth

pull of gravity that changes the path of the Moon

path the Moon would naturally take

Gravity is the force that keeps the Moon orbiting, or circling around, our planet.

The force of gravity also pulls the planets, including Earth, toward the Sun.

planets in their orbits keeps them from falling into the Sun.

On Earth, gravity pulls objects toward the center of the planet. This is what makes objects fall. It is also what keeps objects in place rather than floating around. In order for spacecraft to leave Earth, they must have enough power to overcome the pull of gravity.

COMPARE AND CONTRAST

Compare life on Earth to life without gravity. What would it be like? What might be hard? What might be fun?

ROCKETS

Rockets had been used for many years to shoot fireworks and weapons. In the 1800s people began to think that rockets could be used to launch spacecraft as well.

Rockets carry fuel that is burned inside a chamber. The fuel can be either solid or liquid. The fuel burns when it is mixed with oxygen gas and ignited, or set on fire. As the fuel burns, it gives off a jet of hot

Liquid-Fuel Rocket

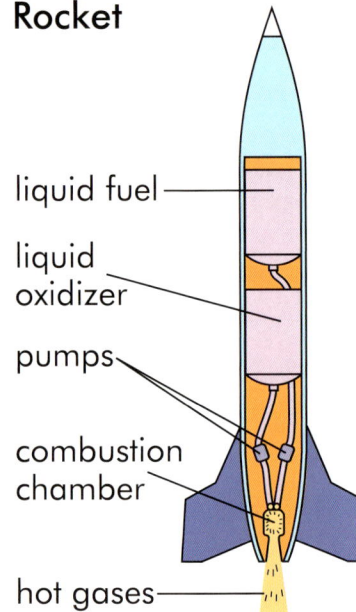

liquid fuel

liquid oxidizer

pumps

combustion chamber

hot gases

Solid-Fuel Rocket

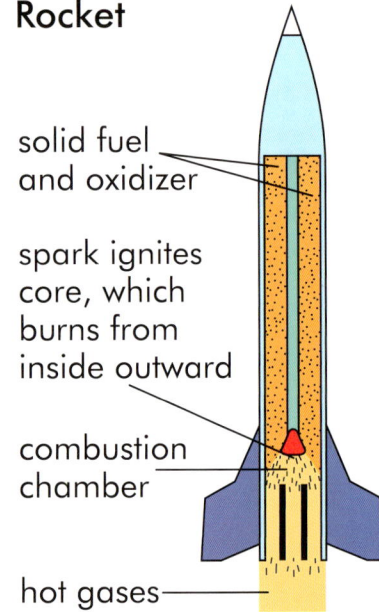

solid fuel and oxidizer

spark ignites core, which burns from inside outward

combustion chamber

hot gases

Rockets carry either solid or liquid fuel. They also carry their own oxygen supply.

Rockets are used to launch satellites and other spacecraft.

Propulsion means the action of propelling, or pushing forward.

gas that shoots out from an opening at the back of the chamber. The force of the gas moving backward pushes the rocket forward. This action is called jet propulsion.

The engines of a jet airplane work in a similar way to rockets. But jet engines get their oxygen from the air. Rockets carry their own oxygen supply. This makes rockets valuable in outer space, where there is no oxygen.

Scientist Robert Goddard experimented with the first modern rockets. He launched the first liquid-fueled rocket from his aunt's farm in Auburn, Massachusetts, in 1926. In the 1930s and 1940s people worked on making rockets more powerful. Many rockets were used as weapons during World War II (1939–45).

In the 1950s scientists began to develop rockets to use for spacecraft. It takes a great deal of power to reach the required speed of at least 25,000 miles (40,000 kilometers) per hour to escape Earth's gravity. The rockets that launch spacecraft are therefore very large. The Saturn V rocket built in the 1960s was 363 feet (111

The space shuttle was a vehicle that was launched into space by rockets but then landed like an airplane when it returned.

▶▶

THINK ABOUT IT

Most of the fuel onboard a rocket is used in the first few minutes of a mission. Why?

space shuttle (U.S.)

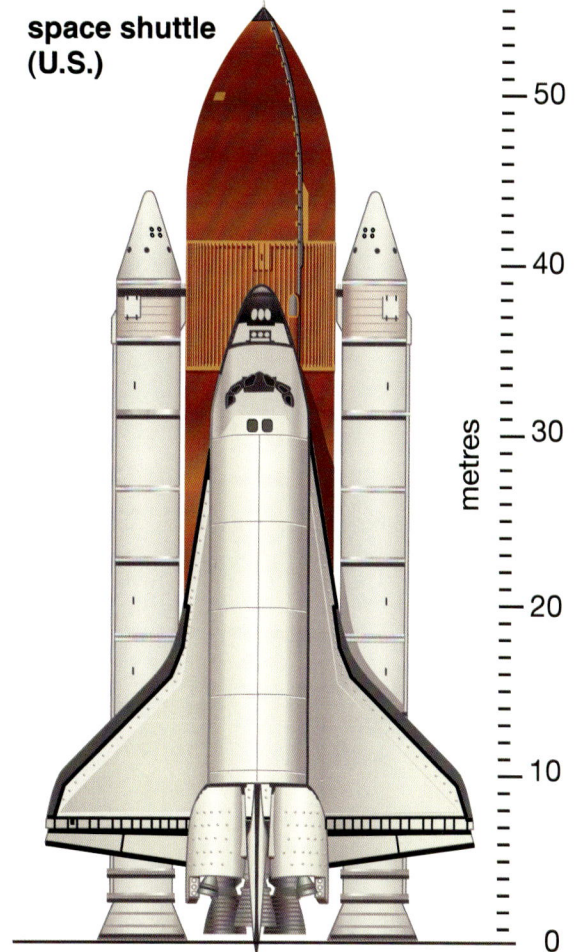

metres

50

40

30

20

10

0

© 2013 Encyclopædia Britannica, Inc.

meters) tall. Today's spacecraft may use more than one type of rocket. One type may be used to launch the spacecraft and another to move it around once it is on its way.

Surrounded by Satellites

A satellite is a small object that orbits a larger object in space. Satellites can be natural or artificial (made by people). The Moon is a natural satellite of Earth. Artificial satellites are sent into space to gather information. Most are launched into space by rockets.

The first artificial satellite was Sputnik 1. The Soviet Union launched Sputnik into orbit around Earth in 1957. The first successful U.S. satellite was Explorer 1, which was launched in 1958. Now dozens of new satellites are put into space every year.

Sputnik 1, about the size of a beach ball, was launched by the Soviet Union in 1957.

There are so many satellites in space that in 2009, two satellites—one American and one Russian—crashed into each other!

Scientific satellites collect information about space. Communications satellites help send telephone calls, radio and

A man-made satellite orbits Earth. Satellites have many purposes.

television programs, and computer information around the world. Airplanes, ships, and cars can use information from satellites to find the way from place to place. Militaries use satellites for spying. Satellites are used in weather forecasting, too.

THE SPACE RACE

After the Soviet Union launched Sputnik 1, the United States increased its space research. Both the United States and the Soviet Union wanted to be the first nation to put a person in space. This became known as the Space Race.

The National Aeronautics and Space Administration (NASA) took charge of the U.S. effort. NASA began Project Mercury in 1958. The goals were to put a spacecraft in orbit with a man onboard, to see how

The Mercury Seven astronauts were presented by NASA on April 9, 1959.

American astronaut Alan B. Shepard, Jr., exits the Mercury spacecraft after his return on May 5, 1961.

a human could function in space, and to return the man and spacecraft safely.

The Soviet Union was the first country to send a human into space. The cosmonaut Yuri Gagarin flew a single orbit around Earth aboard Vostok 1 on April 12, 1961. Shortly after that, on May 5, 1961, astronaut Alan B. Shepard, Jr., became the first American to enter space. Shepard flew for only 15 minutes and did not complete an orbit around Earth.

A Russian astronaut is called a **cosmonaut.**

PROJECT GEMINI

With Project Mercury, the United States successfully sent a man into space and returned him safely. The follow-up, Project Gemini, was announced in January 1962. The goal was to learn even more about how humans can function and survive in space for longer periods of time. It also allowed astronauts to learn how to control a spacecraft in flight.

The Gemini spacecraft had room for two astronauts. Its

A Gemini spacecraft was photographed in orbit 160 miles (257 km) above Earth in December 1965.

On June 3, 1965, Ed White became the first American to perform a spacewalk.

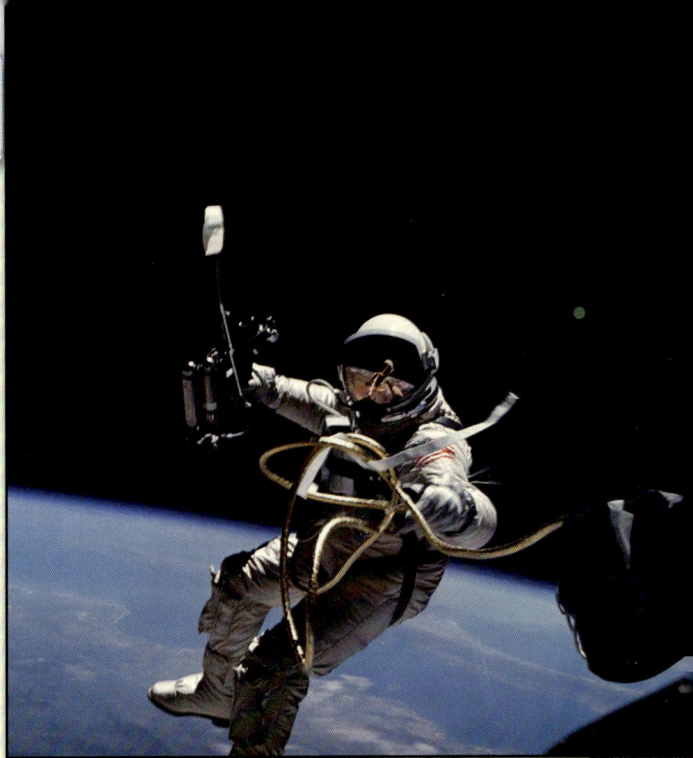

missions helped scientists learn how astronauts could travel outside a spacecraft in a spacesuit. They also learned how to connect two spacecraft together in space.

The first manned Gemini flight was Gemini 3 on March 23, 1965. Virgil I. Grissom and John W. Young completed three orbits of Earth. During the flight of Gemini 4, later in 1965, Edward H. White II became the first American to walk in space, although it was more floating than walking.

THINK ABOUT IT

When going on space walks, astronauts must be fastened to safety tethers. Otherwise, they would float away into deep space.

PROJECT APOLLO

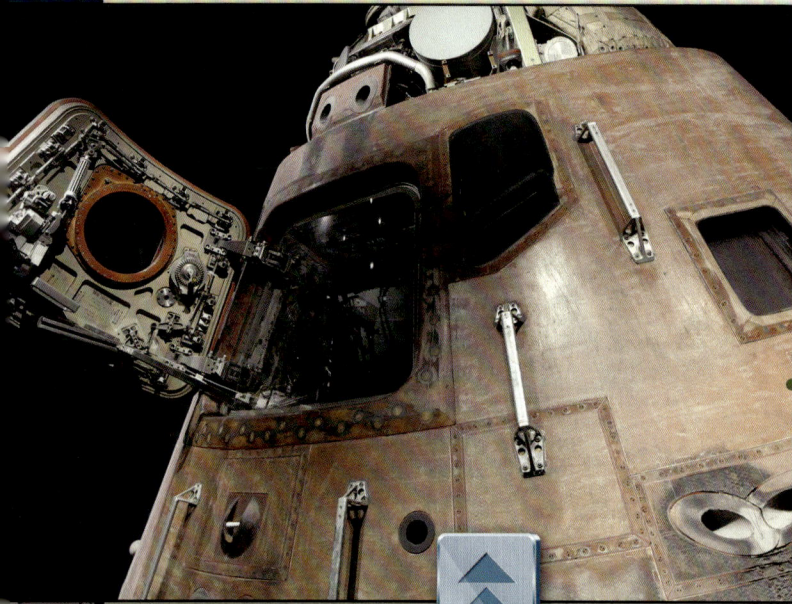

From 1961 to 1975, Project Apollo accomplished 11 spaceflights and the first Moon walk. The Apollo astronauts rode in a section called the command module. The Apollo spacecraft was larger than the spacecraft previously used for the Mercury and Gemini programs.

On July 16, 1969, Neil Armstrong, Edwin E. (Buzz) Aldrin, Jr., and Michael Collins left for the Moon on the Apollo 11 mission. Four days later, Armstrong and Aldrin moved from the command

The Apollo command module is on display at the Kennedy Space Center.

module to a smaller vehicle called the lunar module. The lunar module, also called the *Eagle*, then separated from the rest of the craft. Armstrong and Aldrin flew the *Eagle* to the surface of the Moon. Armstrong became the first person to step onto the Moon. For more than two hours Armstrong and Aldrin collected samples of Moon rocks and soil, made measurements, and took photographs before they began their return trip to Earth.

THINK ABOUT IT

Why do you think the astronauts brought back samples of the Moon's surface?

During the Apollo 11 mission, astronaut Buzz Aldrin planted the American flag on the Moon.

Exploring Deep Space

Space probes are vehicles that carry scientific equipment but no passengers. Some make one-way voyages into deep space. Probes are controlled from Earth by radio. They send back their findings the same way. The probes gather pictures and other information about planets and distant parts of the solar system.

This photo illustration shows the Philae lander on a comet. The lander had separated from the Rosetta probe *(right)*.

In the late 1950s the Soviet Union and the United States launched their first deep-space probes. Probes eventually landed on the planets Mars and Venus and flew past the planets Jupiter, Saturn, Uranus, and Neptune. They collected information on the planets' atmospheres, moons, and ring systems. In the early 2000s scientists sent several new probes to explore Mars and other planets and objects in space. The probes that did not land on planets or other bodies are still traveling through space.

In 2011, NASA launched MESSENGER to study Mercury's surface.

Mars Landers

A lander is a spacecraft designed to rest on the surface of a planet or other body in space. They gather information about the planet and send the information back to Earth.

Several landers have been sent to the surface of Mars in order to explore the planet more closely. In 1975 Viking 1 was the first American spacecraft to touch the surface of Mars. It was also the first spacecraft ever to remain there. It followed a series of short-lived Soviet probes that either landed or crashed into the surface.

The lander Viking I captured this color panorama image of Mars.

In 2004, Mars Exploration Rovers Spirit and Opportunity landed on opposite sides of the planet Mars.

It is difficult to land a probe on the surface of a planet safely. The Mars Exploration Rovers (which landed in 2004) were protected by large airbags. The airbags provided a softer landing by making them a bit like large bouncing balls.

THINK ABOUT IT

On average, Mars is 140 million miles (225 million km) away from Earth. How long do you think it would take to travel there?

THE SPACE SHUTTLE PROGRAM

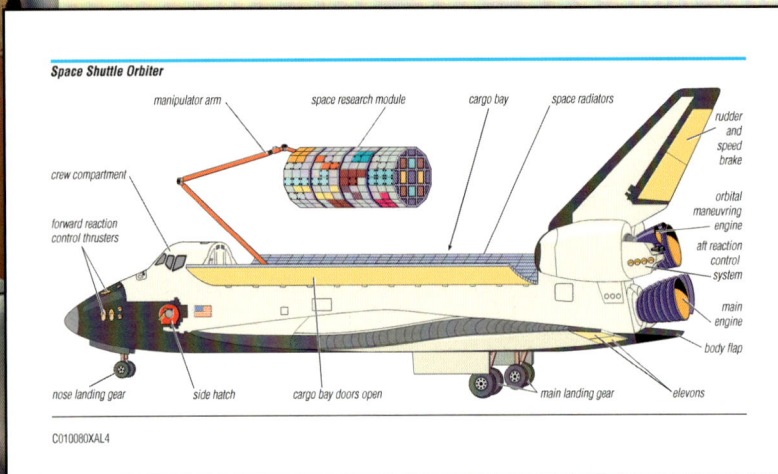

Space Shuttle Orbiter

manipulator arm

space research module

cargo bay

space radiators

rudder and speed brake

orbital maneuvring engine

aft reaction control system

main engine

body flap

elevons

main landing gear

cargo bay doors open

side hatch

nose landing gear

forward reaction control thrusters

crew compartment

C010080XAL4

A diagram shows many parts of a space shuttle orbiter, the reusable part of the spacecraft.

In 1981 NASA launched the first space shuttle, or reusable spacecraft. The main section had wings and was called the orbiter. Attached to the orbiter were rockets, fuel tanks, and oxygen tanks. These boosted the craft through the thickest part of Earth's atmosphere. The shuttles had space for as many as seven astronauts to live and work. They also had a large cargo area. At the end of a mission, the orbiter returned to Earth and landed like an airplane.

There were five shuttles altogether, but two of them were destroyed in accidents. They made more than 100 flights between 1981 and 2011. Each flight lasted up to about two weeks. The astronauts brought supplies to other spacecraft, repaired satellites, performed experiments, and helped build the International Space Station. NASA ended the shuttle program in 2011.

THINK ABOUT IT

On June 18, 1983, astronaut Sally Ride became the first American woman in space.

The seven astronauts onboard died when the *Challenger* space shuttle exploded after liftoff on January 28, 1986.

International Space Station

A space station is a spacecraft in a fixed orbit around Earth. Astronauts can live on a space station for months at a time to gather scientific data and conduct experiments.

The Soviets launched the world's first space station, Salyut 1, on April 19, 1971. The United States launched its first space station, Skylab, on May 14, 1973. It lasted six years.

In the 1990s several countries worked together to

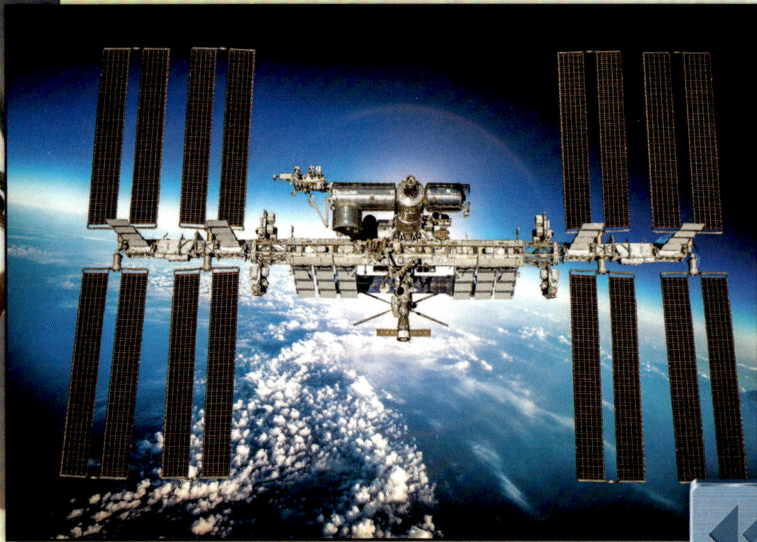

The International Space Station is seen hovering over Earth.

design and build the International Space Station (ISS). The first part of the space station was placed in orbit in 1998. Other parts were added later. Astronauts from many countries now take turns living and working on the ISS.

In space travel the effects of gravity are not felt as they are on Earth. Anything that is not tied down will float around a spacecraft. Those who live on the ISS have to learn how to move through the craft, and they sleep in bags that are mounted on the wall.

A NASA astronaut works onboard the International Space Station.

COMPARE AND CONTRAST

How would your life be different if you lived on a space station?

MISSION TO MARS

The research being done on the International Space Station is helping scientists understand what they need to do to send humans into other parts of outer space. In the 2020s NASA plans to capture and redirect an **asteroid** so that it will orbit the Moon. As it is orbiting the Moon, astronauts can explore the asteroid and also test new systems in human spaceflight.

A drawing shows what a settlement on Mars might look like if astronauts travel there in the future.

An **asteroid** is a small, rocky body that orbits the Sun.

A computer illustration shows a spacecraft orbiting Earth.

Eventually, NASA hopes to send human missions to Mars. Many things must be accomplished for that to become a possibility. Mars is very far away from Earth. A trip to the planet would take years. Scientists do not know if humans can live that long in space. However, scientists have learned a lot from working on the International Space Station and other spacecraft. They have also learned a great deal about Mars from the Mars rovers. Human exploration of Mars could happen in the very near future.

GLOSSARY

astronaut A person who travels in a spacecraft.

atmosphere A layer of gases that surrounds a planet.

data Facts that are collected and studied.

deep space Space outside Earth's atmosphere and especially that part lying beyond the Earth-Moon system.

experiment A procedure or operation carried out under controlled conditions in order to discover something, to test a hypothesis, or to serve as an example.

exploration The act of investigating an unknown area.

launch To send off an object, especially with force.

NASA The National Aeronautics and Space Administration, the space agency of the United States.

orbit The path taken by one body circling around another body.

probe An unmanned spacecraft that explores objects in space and transmits data back to Earth.

rover A space vehicle built to move across the surface of a planet or other body in space.

satellite A small object that orbits a larger object in space.

solar system A star with the group of heavenly bodies that revolve around it.

space The region beyond Earth's atmosphere.

space station A spacecraft in a fixed orbit around Earth.

spacesuit A special suit designed to allow an astronaut to survive in space.

space walk Any physical movement of an astronaut outside a spacecraft in space.

tether A line by which something is fastened so as to limit its range.

For More Information

Books

Aguilar, David. *Space Encyclopedia: A Tour of Our Solar System and Beyond.* Washington, D.C.: National Geographic Children's Books, 2013.

Dale, Penny. *Dinosaur Rocket.* London, England: Nosy Crow, 2014.

Dickinson, Terrance. *Hubble's Universe: Greatest Discoveries and Latest Images.* Richmond Hill, ON, Canada: Firefly Books, 2014.

DK Editors. *Space!* New York, NY: DK Children, 2015.

Hughs, Catherine. *National Geographic Kids First Big Book of Space.* Washington D.C.: National Geographic Children's Books, 2012.

Websites

Because of the changing nature of Internet links, Rosen Publishing has developed an online list of websites related to the subject of this book. This site is updated regularly. Please use this link to access this list:

http://www.rosenlinks.com/LFO/space

INDEX